With best wishes
Sandy and Helen

This book is dedicated to

❧ SIMON, ROSS & ELANOR ❧

who were the first Sandy audiences.

Sandy the Seal Goes Swimming

Annabel and Duncan were staying with Grandma. They were going swimming at the nearby pool. After breakfast they put their swimming things into a bag and set off for the pool.

They ran to watch all the boys and girls in the water through a window in the wall of the pool area.

Suddenly they heard a voice behind them.

"Well! Bless my soul, if it isn't Annabel and Duncan," – and there was Sandy the Seal.

"Sandy!" cried Annabel. "What are you doing here?"

"Oh, I just swam up the River Forth from Edinburgh," said Sandy. "I've been on a tour of Scotland and I spoke to someone who said this was lovely pool and I thought I'd try it. But what are you doing here?"

"We're staying with Grandma," explained Annabel.

"Hello, Sandy" said Grandma. "How are you?"

"I haven't seen you for ages," said Sandy.

"Now," said Grandma "Let's all get into the pool" and they went to the ticket desk.

"One adult and two children, please" said Grandma "Oh, and one seal."

The man at the desk stared at Sandy, then at Grandma and then back at Sandy again.

"What did you say?" he asked.

"One adult, two children and one seal for swimming," said Grandma patiently.

"A seal?" said the man "A seal?"

"Yes." said Grandma. "Didn't you know seals like swimming?"

"I don't think we have a code on the computer for tickets for seals" said the man whose name badge read "Robert – Happy to Help."

"Now, Robert," said Grandma "I'll be responsible for Sandy. He is a very good swimmer, very well behaved and he loves children." And she smiled at Robert in the way that Annabel knew meant it was really best just to agree with her or she would cause a fuss.

Robert obviously knew that look too because he gulped and pressed a button on the computer and the tickets came out of the printer.

"Do you need a swim nappy at all?" asked Robert

"No, thank you" said Grandma "Everyone is out of nappies."

"I meant for your seal" stuttered Robert.

Sandy had been standing very quietly all this time but now he flippered over and stared at Robert.

"For me?" he exclaimed "I've been in more swimming pools and ponds in my life than you've had hot dinners. I most certainly do not need a swim nappy!"

"You can talk!" cried Robert, astonished.

"Of course I can," said Sandy "and swim and eat fish and balance a ball on my nose. What's wrong with that?"

"Nothing at all" said poor Robert "We just don't have many seals in here."

"You've got a monkey that spouts water, a turtle and a snake in there" said Sandy pointing a flipper at the pool.

"Well, yes" said Robert "but they're made of fibre glass and don't talk back."

"Come on, everyone" said Grandma. "Let's get changed. Sandy, we'll see you in the pool."

They all went through the turnstile and into the changing area.

"I'll wait in the showers" said Sandy and flippered off.

Annabel quickly put on her swimsuit and Grandma helped Duncan to get changed. Then they walked through to the shower room for a quick splash before going into the pool.

"There's a chute!" cried Sandy in delight "And doesn't that monkey look funny with water jets coming out of him like that?"

Annabel liked standing in front of the water jets and feeling the water spout onto her tummy and Duncan liked dodging under them. Sandy decided he liked to drink some of the water and then lie under the jets with them playing on his back.

Annabel couldn't count how many times she had to explain to other children and their parents that Sandy was her friend and that he was in the pool for a swim.

Some babies looked doubtful at first but Sandy borrowed someone's ball and started doing tricks with it and they soon started to laugh at him.

"Let's go on the chute" said Annabel to Sandy.

Annabel climbed easily up the steps to the slide but Sandy had to go slowly until he got the hang of it.

"Right, I'll go first" said Annabel "Then you can follow me."

Annabel sat to go down the chute and splashed into the shallow water at the bottom but seals aren't built the same way so Sandy came down headfirst and slithered right along the bottom of the pool after he landed.

"Phew! That was fun" said Sandy when he surfaced. "Shall we do it again?"

"Would you like to go in the big pool?" asked Grandma after a while.

"Alright," said Sandy, so they all went.

"That's an unusual friend you've got" said a lady in the big pool to Grandma.

"Yes," said Grandma "That's Sandy the Seal. I see you have some dive sticks there for collecting from the bottom of the pool. Could we borrow them so he can dive for them? He'd like that."

And the lady agreed.

"Come on, Sandy," said Grandma and threw the dive sticks into the water. "Let's see if seals really can dive for these things."

"One, two, three, go!" cried Duncan and Sandy dived down under the water.

He stayed down for ages and when he surfaced he didn't bring any of the toys up with him.

"What happened to you?" asked Grandma.

"Oh, I got tired fetching things I couldn't eat," said Sandy "So I left them down there."

"Bother!" said Grandma "I'll have to dive down to get them all to return to that kind lady who lent them to us."

"That's OK," said the lady who had been watching. "My boys will dive for them."

"Oh, good," said Sandy. "In that case, thank you very much. Could we all have one more turn on the chute? Then I really must have something to eat. I'm getting quite hungry."

"I am too," said Duncan.

"Well, have your last slide and we'll see what there is to eat at the café before Sandy has to head off back down the river with the tide," said Grandma.

And at the café, there was fish and chips and ice cream cones for everyone.

"My favourites," said Sandy happily.

GET IN TOUCH

If you'd like to know more about Sandy, email him at sandythesealfromtarbert@gmail.com, or visit his Facebook page at Sandy the Seal, or tweet him @Sandy_the_Seal.